X MARKS THE HEART

DARRAGHA FOSTER

VICTORY WOMAN PRESS

CHAPTER ONE

Columbia Middle School. Near the Canadian border in the Pacific Northwest. Small district. An independent district bordering on becoming a religious charter school. No one wanted that —except those who made the decisions. Situated in a blue state, the district's crimson programs and plans frightened staff. At the helm of the weedkiller-laden grassroots efforts to create a theocracy was the middle school's principal. He and his family had finagled their way in and were fully entrenched. Illuminado was careful. He loved his job as head custodian. If things got bad, he could retire. Early. He had enough invested and in other business endeavors to carry him for the next twenty-five years. He'd move home. To Gibraltar.

Never oblivious, but certainly willing to ignore most of the indoctrinating plans, he smiled and hummed to himself as he mopped up a spill in the school cafeteria. He noticed doe-eyed kitchen staff watching him. So were the lunch supervisors. He had that way about him. Spaniard.

Dark. Forty and fit. And his name...it rolled off the tongue with the appeal of hot chocolate on a winter day.

He'd caught looks from staff before. *Why aren't you a model? Are you a bodybuilder?* "No," he'd reply. "I am a pirate." Sometimes he'd get more questions and he'd explain his lineage. Most of the time the response was nervous laughter. He looked the part. A swashbuckling Casanova-type. But he was not a *blackard*. He was a thoughtful, conservative man who did not love recklessly. *I can't help it if my smile makes them believe the sun rises and sets in my shorts.*

He hadn't had a relationship in months. Eight months. They'd parted amicably, but he knew the relationship would have gone toxic. Their ideologies were too varied. She had been horrified by the actions of his forefather and he couldn't seem to convince her that he wasn't cut from the same sailcloth. He tried. It ended.

He wasn't really looking for companionship. Especially with a coworker. He didn't really drink—so bars were out. Clubs weren't his thing since he didn't want to hobnob with a younger crowd. *Over forty is fine. Give me a mature woman who knows what she wants in life, isn't afraid of having a woman's body, says 'fuck you' to societal norms of beauty and fashion, and likes sex and coffee. I don't ask for much.*

He took his break after all the lunches were over. After swabbing the decks, he left all the lunchroom tables up for the deep clean from the night crew. No need to put them down again for an assembly or afterschool program. The principal had canceled the program because the man hired to run it was polyamorous. No one said that aloud, of course. *But we know. Principal Brown runs a tighter ship than I and he disposes of everything that does not fit into his very narrow schema.*

He didn't always sit in the staff lounge for his break. Sometimes he sat in the courtyard or his office. It was his unpaid time and though he wasn't supposed to leave school grounds, he liked the time spent alone. In silence. Today...however, he'd left his lunch in the staff fridge. There, he found a surprise.

A lovely woman he'd not seen before. He stopped dead in his tracks. The sight of her took his breath away. His arms and legs went numb. His spine tingled. His vision blurred until all he could see was her face. An angel.

Their gazes met. The moment lingered between them like a thick blanket of fog, hiding everything else from view, sweetening the heavy air. He held out his hand. "I am Illuminado Constantine, custodian."

The angel smiled. "Nice to meet you. I'm Saber MacLean."

Illuminado shifted his weight. "You are new?"

Saber nodded. "I've been hired as a long-term substitute teacher to cover for a teacher taking an extended emergency leave."

Illuminado's interest was piqued to a higher level. "Hennessey?"

Saber smiled. "Yes. He left for Guatemala yesterday morning. Seems his son is in a bit of trouble down there. Married a local gal and is refusing to come home."

"You can't stop love. Hennessey will be unsuccessful. I know Latin people and they love very deeply," Illuminado replied. "Hennessey is a widower. I bet he will find love, too. And stay."

"Are you from Central America?" Saber asked. "Your accent…"

"I am from Gibraltar. Born there. My accent comes from my mother's side—she was Spanish. I lived in La Lenea, Spain with my grandparents and cousins every summer until we moved. My father has a very strong British accent, but we most often spoke Spanish in our home, as my mother preferred it. Everyone in Gibraltar speaks English, Spanish, and Llanito—a mixture."

"You're a long way from home."

"Ah, home is where the heart is."

"Do you clean my room?"

"Night crew does."

"Anything I should know? No paperclips left on the floor and staples in the recycle bin, right?"

"Thank you. Take care of your custodian and he shall always take care of your needs, too. Many teachers—they do not understand this. At my last school, there was a man who brought sheep and goats into his classroom. What a nightmare."

———

Like a dry riverbed in a flash flood, Saber felt a chilling heat course down her spine, through her nipples and belly, finally coming to rest in that sensitive place between her legs. His dark eyes and sexy accent were as good as foreplay. "I'll do my best to make sure my room is left in good order at the end of the day, Mr. Constantine. No farm animals, I promise."

"Call me Illuminado," he replied. He took a bite from a roll in his lunch sack.

Saber smiled—and felt her palms sweat and neck heat up. *Jesus Christ. I'm blushing.* "Illuminado."

"Saber. Saber MacLean," Illuminado said softly. "I am very happy to know you. We shall speak again. Your tardy bell comes shortly."

Saber felt a stab in her stomach that reminded her of middle school unrequited love. "I guess I'll see you around, Illuminado. It was nice meeting you," she said, extending her hand.

Illuminado took her hand and held it gently. He smiled, enjoying the flush of her cheeks. With a simple eye movement, he could make a woman want him. It was a Spaniard's way.

CHAPTER TWO

Saber MacLean was the child of professional fencers. Not the kind one builds around a house, but Olympians. She was forty, and had yet to land a permanent contract teaching, so she subbed. A long-term sub job was ideal, as the number of hours she would work would garner benefits. Medical, dental, vision. A burgeoning state retirement plan. She was grateful for the job—even though the principal was super creepy. He stared at her. Dead eyes. A droning voice and several religious décor choices gracing his office. He had a window to the main hall—a two-way mirror. He could see out. Everyone else could see themselves. Undoubtedly all the staff knew about his portal. She wondered if he had other ways to watch students and staff. Hidden cameras. Microphones. All illegal—but he didn't seem to care within the confines of his own personal theocracy.

She signed a code of ethics after accepting the three-month job. Not a district code of ethics—but a school-based one.

I need this job. I never wanted to teach in a right-wing

parochial school, but a paycheck is a paycheck. I can do anything for three months.

She smiled politely and agreed to keep the Ten Commandments poster in her room, prominently displayed. She received a packet of daily Bible verses to share with her classes. And she promised to not participate in lude or lascivious behaviors.

As if. I have a master's degree in K-12 education, a BA in history, and better credentials than what this job calls for. What is his game? I don't want to know anything more about him than his name. I'll do my job, collect my paycheck and credit hours, and keep applying for continuing contract jobs outside this bizarre district in June.

Saber had little interest in romance. The single cat lady scenario worked for her.

CHAPTER THREE

Saber MacLean. Saber MacLean. It is a name like music. I must know her better.

Smitten, Illuminado withheld the urge to dash to Saber's classroom and went through the motions of his day with butterflies in his belly. His custodial cell chirped. Water spill in 111. *The gods smile upon me today! That is her room.*

He wheeled a mop and bucket to the classroom and Saber motioned toward the back without breaking a beat while explaining something to her class. He cleaned up the water spill and then looked for the cause. It wasn't just a kid spill. The sink had a drip above the U-joint. He pulled out his pipe wrench and tightened it barely disturbing the class. He always carried the right tools for the job. The bell rang and the students left for their elective. He stretched.

"Well, problem solved?" Saber asked.

"Nothing a good turn of the right tool can't handle."

"The admin assistant here—she's good. I buzzed her

extension, and you showed up less than five minutes later."

"She is good, indeed. Over twenty years at this school." He paused. "I'll check your pipes later. Make sure nothing else is leaking."

"I hope you will," Saber replied.

Illuminado was loathe to say he heard a tone to her voice that was quite "come hither," but the tone was there, nevertheless. "I'll see you later, Miss McLean."

"And you, Mr. Constantine."

"Miss MacLean...I made paella. After school would you like to join me for dinner? It's a nice day...we can eat in the staff lounge with the door to the courtyard open."

"I'd like that. See you at 4:30."

"See you then." He paused, noticing the volumes of butcher paper and book covers across the back counter. "Are you decorating your classroom?"

"Absolutely. You'll see."

"Indeed, I will. See you soon, Ms. MacLean."

CHAPTER FOUR

He enjoyed his job. He took pride in keeping a safe and tidy school. It became his playground. No...it became his ship of dreams. Illuminado had the blood of a pirate in his veins. As a descendent of Benito de Soto, acts of piracy were a part of his DNA. And he ran a tight ship. When he mopped the halls, he mopped the decks of his forefather's ship, *Burla Negra, the Black Joker.* When he found coins or jewels strewn about, the lost and found box became his treasure chest. The climbing structure in the indoor play shed was his Rock of Gibraltar.

Sometimes he didn't want people to know of his ancestry. Benito de Soto had been a terrible man. He was remembered for his murderous cruelty. Wikipedia was not complimentary. He was a descendant of a son of Benito's by a woman captured and brutalized but left alive. 1827. The family Bible kept it all straight. Generation after generation thrived in the shadow of the Rock, until his parents brought him to America.

He knew of his unfortunate family ties quite young.

Mother scolded him *no actúes con tu sangre, hijo. Do not act on your blood. Do not behave like a rapine pirate. Love Jesus, not the sea.*

He'd converted to Buddhism after leaving home for college and found some inner peace by chanting when his blood boiled. He promised himself he would never commit atrocious acts against any human—especially never to harm women. Benito had no control and reportedly considered women property. It sickened him…and yet he felt that pull sometimes. When angered. When dealing with willful ignorance in others. When the principal offered blessings and prayers without consent. But he kept his cool and did not reave and pillage. He did not murder or take a woman without her consent. He had strong blood ties, but not the temperament, thankfully.

His work wasn't difficult, the pay and benefits were great, and his wandering imagination made his days go quickly as he swabbed the decks and swept away debris in search of buried treasure. Illuminado had a new treasure map to follow now. Her room. *X marks the heart.*

He'd baked a paella and brought the whole clay Dutch-style oven with him to work. His mother had given the pot to him as if it were the most sacred of family artifacts. It had a special shelf in his kitchen and as instructed, he used olive oil to keep it non-stick. *¡Sin lavavajillas! Never put it in a dishwasher.* Per mother.

Making a huge pot of paella was a fortuitous act if ever he'd made one. A good reason to have company for dinner. The saffron fragranced the air as if he were in his mother's kitchen. She knew her spices and loved to feed people. That's where he got it. Food is love. He shot an email out to the night crew indicating that dinner was on him. Paella only tasted better after sitting. He used rabbit and smoked mussels. His mother's secret. The saffron rice grew deeper in color. Orange-yellow-like sunsets over the Strait of Gibraltar. A taste of home.

———

Saber took a hard breath as Illuminado pushed his mop bucket out of her room. *I'm hungry now. Paella, yes. But him...more so. How can I resist the charms of a handsome Spaniard who knows how to clean and sanitize? Lord only knows what the man could do with duct tape!*

Her first full day on the job and the kids were kind to her. But the last bell couldn't sound quickly enough. Middle school was insane but stepping in as a long-term substitute brought added tension to the mix. With spring break days away...the kids were restless. She took the last ten minutes of every class period to take them for a walk. She picked up a radio from the office on her way out the door and kept both eyes on her charges, but her mind... *wandered.* Illuminado. Hotter than a sandy beach in Majorca and far more mysterious than Tangiers across the Strait of Gibraltar.

———

Illuminado pulled his cleaning cart into the custodial closet and parked it. He had a full shaving kit in his locker at the school. He quickly washed his hands and face and brushed his teeth in the sink. He changed out of his coveralls and into a flannel shirt and jeans. He smoothed his thick dark brown hair back into a neat ponytail. He had a whisper of gray in his eyebrows and beard, but his hair had stayed dark. So far.

He switched the staff room oven on to 425 degrees and slid in his clay baking dish full of paella. He dimmed the lights over the sofa and coffee table area and set out two plates, two forks, and two ice-cold bottles of water from the vending machine. The staff lounge was so ugly. Only her presence could make it beautiful. It had orange cabinets and mismatched tile flooring. The carpeted area was threadbare, and one microwave would forever reek of fish after a teacher cooked befouled crabcakes. It did have a view, however. The school sat on a hill overlooking the bay, facing west. Some days the water looked like glass and at other times, a tempest. Across a bridge built in 1912, it was the last school in the city, and near the border to another county. It was too far out to grab the attention of private volleyball clubs and the like. There were few night rentals. And the area in which the school was built was a wealthier neighborhood. The original copper downspouts were intact. A fire destroyed part of the original building in 1901. Subsequent additions and remodels had left it a jumbled maze of classrooms. It even had an interior courtyard inaccessible by any means save a single door at the back of the commons. Odd design. He imagined that before the 1912 bridge, children rode their horses or were put into carts and driven by their parents. One or two of the original hitching posts remained.

He patted his forehead nervously. "*Necesito una vela,*" he mumbled. "Where are the damned candles?" There were birthday cake candles in the silverware drawer. They'd have to do. Not very romantic, but when having one minute to set a mood, any candle would do.

The school was eerily empty. Of course...it was Friday. Only the night crew remained. No sports. No activities.

Even the office staff had ducked out a little early. His ship of dreams was about to make port.

"Illuminado?" Saber called.

"*Si, Seniorita. Te aguardo aquí,*" he replied softly. "I am here."

Saber giggled. "*Gracias, Senior.*" She paused as she entered the break room. "Oh, my. Candlelight and what is that heavenly aroma?"

Illuminado chuckled. "Welcome to my mother's own recipe carried to America in her little handbag. I was a teenager, always hungry, and knew that once we were settled, Mother would bring out the clay pot and make paella for me. It is a food of celebration."

"You immigrated as a teen?" Saber asked.

"We came from Gibraltar when I was fourteen. My family home is in the shadow of the Rock. I still have relatives in the Andalusian region."

"*Here be monsters. Ne plus ultra. Go no further or no more beyond,* warned the Romans," Saber replied. "The Rock of Gibraltar was once hailed as a pillar of Hercules and the ends of the earth. To sail beyond it meant certain doom."

Illuminado laughed. "This is true. Many offerings to the gods have been found on Gibraltar. They hoped to still the seas and tame the beasts that lay beyond. Of course, the only true monsters are those in our minds— and they can be quite fierce."

Saber sighed. Dinner with a hot Spaniard with burning charcoal eyes, a sexy accent—and a job.

"My paella. Please, be seated." Illuminado motioned toward the sofa.

"So, tell me about growing up in the shadow of the Rock of Gibraltar," Saber asked.

"Tell me how you got the first name of *Saber*," Illuminado replied.

"You first." She opened her water bottle.

"I shall speak while I serve our dinner, how's that?" Illuminado began. "I have stood at the top of the world. From the top of the Rock of Gibraltar you have Europe at your feet. Africa fills one horizon, while the gates to the Mediterranean and the Atlantic are on either side. One understands why the Rock and its sister Mount Hacho in Morocco are called the Pillars of Hercules and are sacred sites in myth and legend. When I marry, it shall be at the top of the Rock, God's most holy site."

"You're getting married?" Saber asked, hoping the disappointment she felt wasn't reflected in her voice.

"Not yet. First I must find a bride."

Relief! "What did your parents do in Gibraltar?" she asked.

"Mother worked for the Brits as a bookkeeper and Father ran the tram to the top of the Rock."

"It sounds very romantic. Why did your parents move here?"

"First, tell me of Saber MacLean," Illuminado commanded softly, reaching a serving spoon into the clay pot.

The room filled with the scents of baked rice, saffron, and olive oil as he scooped the decadent dish onto their plates.

"I'd better give you an explanation for my name now because I think I may go into some kind of rapturous state after taking the first bite of your paella. Chicken? Sausage?"

Illuminado smiled. "Rabbit."

"Rabbit?" Saber questioned.

"I told you this is my mother's recipe. Don't worry. Rabbit is the other white meat. With a name like Saber, you aren't afraid of trying something new, are you?"

"My mother and father were championship fencers. I grew up at the point of a rapier. I'm Saber after their art. I changed the spelling from S A B R E to S A B E R to make life easier. Father is Scottish and I thank God every day he didn't name me *Claymore*. One of my brothers, however, did not escape that fate. My brothers are Claymore and Falchion. Twins. And I've eaten rabbit before."

Illuminado poked his fork into the rice. "I love the color of the rice. Such a perfect golden yellow saffron makes it. Please, take a bite, my woman of steel."

Saber slid her fork into the golden mound of rice and finely chopped vegetables, her mouth watering. The first bite sent cascades of flavor throughout her body. "Oh, my God."

"Is good, no?" Illuminado teased.

"Oh, my God," Saber repeated.

"Mother would be pleased with your reaction." Illuminado took a bite of his paella, and suddenly felt the urge to join in Saber's prayer. "*Jesus Cristo. Es delicioso.*"

"You can say that again," Saber replied. "So, Illuminado, other than your mother, there is no Mrs. Constantine?"

"Correct. And I assume there is no Mr. MacLean?"

"Only my father and brothers." Saber agreed. "I just turned forty. My brothers are two years younger. One is an Olympian and the other is a cameraman for the various survival shows."

"Well, my dear Saber, then if only your father and brothers claim the name, we shall have to have another date," Illuminado replied.

"Another?"

"I looked at you and knew we must become friends. I want to know you. I am of the Iberian Peninsula. Spanish. Gibralterian. We live and love passionately."

"Oh, my."

"You stir feelings here," he placed his hand atop his heart. "I have not had such a fire in my chest for a very long time. I do not want to frighten you, but I must get to know you. Please forgive my forward conversation. I know it is against school policy for us to date. Not against district policy—but only that of our current administrator. But he cannot still a beating heart."

"Well, I suggest a coffee shop and a long chat. Tell me...why does Mr. Brown forbid romance?"

"He is a man with a broken heart and too many rules in his life. I think they make him feel safe. His wife and children abandoned him and this new church he attends...*creo que es engañoso*. It is very strict."

"*Engañoso?*" Saber Googled the words on her phone. "Ah, deceptive. Well, that will never do, will it? Is it fundamentalist evangelical?"

Illuminado nodded. "*Si*. Very controlling. He is under their spell and sets forth conditions for his staff based on his new belief system. I don't think anyone has ever turned him in to the district because no one cares enough about him to help. Plus, his brother is superintendent and he has two cousins on the board. And yet...he is alone. I think it is best if you maintain a distance from him and if at all possible, never be alone in a room with him. I'll explain more later." He reclined. He studied Saber's gentle motions of fork to plate and fork to mouth. He wanted to be that lucky fork, encircled by her soft lips; tasted by her warm tongue. "Saber," he whispered.

"Yes?"

I want to rip your clothes off and make love to you as no man has ever made love to you before. I can give you orgasms better than how my paella tastes. "I am glad you have joined me for dinner today."

Saber withheld a crestfallen pout. *Why doesn't he just rip my clothes off and do me over the coffee table?* "I am sorry that he has alienated himself so much. On a brighter note, I finished my room decorations today."

"Ah, what is your theme?" Illuminado asked.

"Pirates. I know it's not in the curriculum, but it is a history class."

"You like pirates? That's good. Very good. I know a pirate."

Saber reached for their dishes. "I know a pirate, too. And the pirate I know...is me. I am a descendant of Calico Jack Rackham and his dalliance with Anne Bonny. She escaped the gallows by pleading the belly after being enriched by Jack. She bore him a son whose descendant is me."

Illuminado nearly jumped out of his skin. *Set sail with me, beautiful Saber.* "I am born of the line of Benito de Soto, born in 1800. Spaniard and pirate." He paused. "He was a very defiant, hard-headed man. Rather than allow somebody to hang him, he stood on top of his coffin held in a cart and calmly reached for the gallows, and adjusted the noose around his own neck. It is said he smiled at the gathered crowd and exclaimed "*Adios Todos!*" as he jumped from the cart to his slow painful death. Even as he met death, he was braver than most men are in life."

"We share a rich history, sir." She waved her hand dramatically. "Rich, indeed."

He grabbed her hand and touched his lips to it. It wasn't enough. He wanted more of her.

———

She sighed as Illuminado turned her hand over and planted a kiss on the pulse point of her wrist. Her eyes rolled back and she felt her female parts blossom with readiness. Her hand still in his, she leaned forward, lifting her chin. They were so close she could feel his heat against her cheeks. One slight movement and their lips could touch. "I need dessert." She breathed the words into his mouth as their lips met.

The electricity of their joined hands arced. A short, but passionate kiss. There was no sweeter or more fitting dessert to a dinner of paella.

"Thank you," Saber whispered against Illuminado's lips. "I should be heading home soon. I've got...things to plan..."

"I understand. Can we meet tomorrow? Coffee?"

Saber nodded. "I'd like that. I'd really like that."

"We have a weekend, Saber MacLean. Shall we set sail?"

"Hoist the colors. Hold steady."

"We have made a compact," Illuminado replied. "Noon at the shop down the street? The one with the lighthouse."

"I love that place." She stood and backed away slowly, then turned and left the break room as calmly as she could. As soon as she knew she was out of sight and earshot, she let loose with a maniacal giggle of pure delight.

Illuminado felt drugged. Drugged by the embrace of

an angel. *Muerto e ido al cielo. I am dead and gone to heaven. She is heaven. I could love this woman.*

She had to pick up her work bag from her room. Sounds carried in the empty school, and from its opposite end, she heard a soft hum coming from the corridor. It was a familiar tune. A sea shanty. A pirate's song.

Gobsmacked, he realized he hadn't asked for her number. The urge to text her was overwhelming. To carry on their conversation. All evening. "Wait!" He dashed through the empty school, mobile phone in hand. "What is your number?"

Saber stopped and held out her phone. "Airdrop?"

"Si," he replied.

And numbers were exchanged.

"And now, sir, our compact is complete," Saber replied. She glanced at her phone. Probably the most important number she'd ever entered was now in her contacts. Illuminado Constantine. Spaniard. Custodial pirate.

CHAPTER FIVE

The cute, nautical-themed coffee house a block away from the school might not be the best place to meet. Students. Other staff. But on a Saturday, her fears were assuaged. The place was buzzing, but with a crowd she decidedly did not know. Early, she bought a cup and chose a table in the far back corner. She could see the entrance from the parking lot. At one minute to twelve, Illuminado quietly entered. *Oh, he's a looker. Gazes are upon him. Some stares lasting longer than others. His eyes are so dark they appear ringed by liner. His hair has only the slightest hint of gray and he walks...he walks as if he owned the place.*

He strolled to her—never casting his gaze in any other direction. It almost unnerved her. Almost.

"Hello, Saber."

"Hello Illuminado. Please...get a cup and join me."

He pulled out a chair and nestled beside her. Not across from her. Beside. "The barista knows my drink. She'll bring it to me."

"Are they all in love with you? The way people stop and stare..."

"In love with me? No. Curious? Yes. And I tip well. Profit sharing. Truthfully, when I want my coffee, I don't want to wait, so I pre-order on their app. It helps that I am the owner, too."

"The owner? Well, you are full of surprises. Is going to the counter to order for peasants?"

Illuminado reached his arm around her shoulders and drew her in for a kiss. Again...short...but passionate. "We are the descendants of sea-faring royalty. We need not wait for anything."

"I bet you can quote from *Pirates of the Caribbean*." Saber didn't pull away. Face to face with Illuminado, she took a deep breath and exhaled it against his neck. "I feel the need to tell you I do take what I want—but am generous in exchange."

"*Mi belleza*. I have always been cautious with my affections. Never too close to home, if you know what I mean. But you make me *deseosa*. We may work together, but such attraction as this cannot be ignored. Come home with me. Now." He flicked her ear with his tongue. "I will pleasure you. Put myself to you until we are spent. Drink in all parts of you. Taste you."

"I will make port with you, Illuminado." A decision quickly made. It seemed right. It felt as though nothing in heaven or earth could sway her from lying with him.

"Let's bring our coffees and walk to my home."

"I can leave my car here?" Saber asked.

"Yes. It will be fine."

"How do you know?" Saber asked.

"As I said, I am the owner."

"Is your place close?"

"It is."

"All right."

Illuminado held her hand as they exited the shop with their coffees. Around the back of the store, he pulled out a key and opened what Saber had always thought was a docking bay for freight—which it was. However, there was a small elevator just inside. They took it to the top floor of the shop, under a false lighthouse complete with glow—and a condo.

"You live in a lighthouse."

"I have a three-bedroom, two-bath apartment above the shop with access to the lighthouse—which has the best view of the city to be had. I have a home in the country, too—but this is closer to work."

"A gentleman pirate with a country home."

"Yes? Can I help you, madam? But do not be overly excited about my place by the lake. It is a tiny home. Less than six hundred square feet." Illuminado pulled Saber in tight as they rode the lift upwards. This kiss lasted. Prelude to the act. Tongues gently touching. Lips pressing. He had a five o'clock shadow and the whisker burn aroused her as he kissed her throat and opened her blouse to bury his face in her cleavage.

I need him now. She held his head to her breasts. *I need him in me, right now. I am going to fuck the living daylights out of him as soon as we get into his apartment. Right now.*

The lift door opened into a foyer inlaid with marble. She didn't give him a moment to welcome her. She pulled Illuminado to the cold floor and straddled him, fumbling with his buckle and zipper. *He has Roman tile. I see Roman tile and an old saber.* "Oh, Gods...yes." *He's hard. So hard.* She raised herself up a little, hiked up her skirt, and slid back her panties. With no other foreplay, she used her hand to guide him inside her ready quim. She pressed down, taking as much of him as she could.

He arched his back and held her hips in place. "*No quiero parar. Oh Dios.* Saber, protection. We should use protection."

"Oh, fuck it!" She rolled off. "Is it real? The tile?"

"Yes. It is real. It is leftover from the shower installation in my family home in Gibraltar. It was unearthed at the turn of the 19th century, pulled up, stacked up, and forgotten until I took control of things. But do you really want to talk about tile? I have condoms in the next room. Come with me."

Saber didn't know what to say. There were no words for her desires. She growled.

Ah, she has lost human speech under my touch. Illuminado led her into the living room and stripped.

———

She didn't think she could get out of her clothing quickly enough. He sat on the couch with his impressive woody in his hand. He wasn't a grandiose length. Probably average. But he was thick. *Thick is good. And anything over six inches is wasted.* She stood before him, unashamed of her forty-plus years reflected in her body. He pulled her closer and leaned in to lick her clitoris. She pushed his head into her labia. He parted her pussy lips and slowly slid a finger into her. She began to rock to the rhythm he set with probing laps and fingers.

The heat built and every nerve in her body seemed to begin and end at that sensitive nub between her legs. He lapped in long strokes from vagina to apex and held her fast. "You're going to make me cum." He made a throaty noise as she rocked herself against his face and climaxed.

He pulled away and grabbed her hips and rammed his cock inside her as she straddled him on the sofa. She hadn't seen him put on the condom. *Fuck...I wouldn't have noticed an earthquake.* She rocked her hips and pushed her clit against his pelvic bone over and over until the flower of orgasm built within her a second time. She watched his face, scrunched with pleasure. She bore down. He could go no further into her. Where his body began and hers ended...gone. They were one.

––––––––

Illuminado wanted to hold fast. Hold his orgasm. The condom had done nothing to quell his passion as they are known to do. He held her hips and kept her fixed atop his lap as he came. He breathed into her breasts and squeezed her buttocks as he surged. It pleased him that a moment later, she uttered something so guttural and deep that he knew she had achieved orgasm a second time.

Saber fell onto her side on the sofa. Illuminado rose and stripped off the condom. "Be right back," he whispered.

He returned to find her wrapped up in a crocheted Afghan he'd tossed over the back of his couch. "You are magnificent."

"As are you."

He kissed her, then crawled under the soft throw with her. "I would like to make love to you slowly."

"And I'd like you to bend me over the window ledge of the lighthouse and nail the shit out of me. I want you to fuck my ass. I want to swallow your cock. I want to do things to you that are unspeakable. Don't be too surprised. You bring it out in me." *Oh, gods. I am talking dirty. He brings out something in me. And I feel safe. It's okay to say and do exactly what I want. With him.*

"I am not surprised or concerned. I hope we will have a healthy sex life. I promise you...I will take you in the turret. In the loading dock. After hours atop the barista's service bar. I will put my tongue deep inside you and withdraw from you the nectar of the gods then use it to lubricate your ass and I will fuck you deeply. I will fuck your mouth. I will bring you many climaxes. This, I shall do."

Saber straightened her back. *This is foreplay...* "And I will suck you dry and finger your ass. I will lick your balls and suck on your tongue like it is your cock. I will ride you until you scream and masturbate while you fuck my ass—using a vibrator in my pussy so that when you shoot your load into me, I, too, will come."

"Should we have a snack first?" He laughed.

"Yes. Let's make something. Have any leftover paella?"

Illuminado nodded toward his kitchen. "Of course. Let me reheat it. But no microwave. It ruins the flavor." He stood and walked nude toward the fridge. "I like the way you talk to me. It is good to know a woman who is not afraid to tell me exactly what she wants to do."

"I have no problem being exceedingly verbal—especially where my pleasure is concerned. I quit playing games and figured that if more women spoke up about what we want in the sack, peace on earth might become a reality."

"All the things you say to do, we will do. Maybe not

today. What we don't accomplish this afternoon we shall do tomorrow. As long as we can walk into work Monday." He paused as he prepared the food. "Saber...I had a vasectomy a few years ago. It is reversible should I ever want children, but I was not going to leave it up to my partners to provide protection. And my union check-up showed I am disease-free."

"I have an IUD and my last exam was a month ago. I'm clean as a whistle."

"*Perfecto*. If you wish we can dispense with the condoms since we cannot conceive and we will be sharing passion only, no disease."

"I'm game if you are." Saber strolled into the kitchen. She liked how she looked. According to the misogynistic BMI scale, she was overweight. Screw that. Hard.

"I have not often had a naked beauty in my kitchen," Illuminado said, encircling his arms around her waist.

Saber reached for his cock. "I want you again. Now."

"Before the paella?"

She dropped to her knees and swallowed his penis. Saber stroked it into her mouth, her tongue playing with the foreskins. *He's so hard. And his penis is so beautiful. Perfect.*

Jutting out from him like the limb of a tree with a healthy circumference to stretch her open in all manners of pleasurable ways, his cock responded to her touch. "*Bella*...I would have you."

"If I suck you off how long will it take you to get hard again?"

"It has been a very long time since I last made love to a woman. Please, let me have you. Fill you. I want you to come with the weight of my body atop you and I will be spent deep inside you."

"Gods, how can a woman refuse such poetry?" She laid back on the tile floor and reached for her clit. "Come on." She continued masturbating as he laid down upon her and guided his hardness into her ready pussy. She didn't move her hand. She continued pushing and pulling on her clitoris as he pumped. She raised her legs higher and wrapped them around his hips. "Fuck me harder." She pushed an orgasm out as he fucked her hard and deep. She giggled as his body shook and he groaned. "That's right, mister. Come inside me. Fill me."

"I have. *Te follé profundamente.* Gods, Saber. You are the best I've ever had."

CHAPTER SIX

Their snack was rushed, but tasty.

"This is so good. I'm glad you had leftovers. I worked up an appetite."

"I'm glad you enjoy all my offerings. You know...I have a steam shower. Would you like to have a go? Maybe a kiss and fondle?"

Saber nodded. "Where is it?"

"It is in the lighthouse."

"No shit."

"It is very nice."

Saber touched his cheek. "Good Lord, you're amazing."

"Yes, I am. But Saber...will you see me outside places we can make love? Can I take you to dinner? To a concert? Sporting event?"

"Of course. But know this, sir...I will fuck you when I want and wherever I can. You say it's been a while since you made love to a woman...it's been well over a year for me."

"To a woman?"

Saber laughed. "To a man. But I have had women."

"And I have been with men. It is the lover in me. But I prefer women. One woman."

"I'm glad. If you're looking for a monogamous relationship, I'm your girl."

Illuminado leaned forward and kissed her. "That is my goal. You. Just you."

Saber whispered against his lips, "I want you inside me again, Illuminado."

"Never let me stop you from achieving your goals."

———

The tower steam room was accessed by a pull-down ladder in his bedroom. Amazingly, the room below the timed flashing light was well-appointed. Carpet. A small sink and toilet. A jet fridge, a settee, and a gorgeous shower.

"This is amazing. Do you relax up here?"

"I do. From the panel, I can control the color and speed of the lighthouse, too. I can play a foghorn—but the neighbors don't like the noise."

He turned on the shower. Dual head, porcelain, with the ability to spray from ankle to crown. The steam enticed them to caresses and they explored each other's bodies in the mist.

"Come along, *mi amor*." Illuminado stepped into the mist and extended his hand to steady Saber as she entered. They kissed as desperately as their first. Ardor overwhelmed them. Their tactile exploration continued. Saber ran her fingers along his backside as he slipped clever fingers between her legs.

"I smell lavender."

"Yes. I can make scents. I built this in when I remod-eled for the coffee shop."

"You built all this?"

"*Si.* Carpentry, plumbing, electrical. I can do it all. Masonry, too. My father and mother saw to my practical education."

"I am impressed."

He encircled her tightly then suddenly turned her so that her back was to his belly. "What was this about your rear end?"

"Oh, yes. Do you have lube?"

"Olive oil. In the recessed niche to your left."

"That will work."

Illuminado reached for the stone pump dispenser of olive oil and filled his palm before stroking it onto his dick, as he had done numerous times in his shower for self-enjoyment. Saber knelt against the bench and he positioned himself behind her. He slicked her anus with his olive oil-soaked member and entered her slowly. She pushed against him so that he went solidly in. She moaned and gave verbal encouragement that nearly made him blush. "Fuck me harder! Come on. Come on. I want to feel your hotness deep inside me."

"I will do what I can," Illuminado chuckled.

Saber came before he did. She masturbated to climax and as her pleasure ebbed and flowed, he orgasmed.

"I am spent, Saber."

"Yes." She hadn't risen from her position hunched over the bench seat yet. "Coffee. I need coffee."

"Easily done. The owner of the shop below...I know him."

They showered and dressed and strolled into the coffee shop like proud cats. Wet hair and no makeup,

Saber felt a little naked, but damn...anyone who saw them would probably figure she'd had a better day than they did. *I feel like my insides have been pushed up into my chest cavity. That was some damned fine sex.*

"French press, whipping cream, turbinado sugar." Illuminado looked around. "Table three."

The barista nodded. "Yes, sir."

Saber took his arm as they walked to their table. "Sir?"

"Not mandatory. Just respect. I pay well and my benefits are second to none. We are a union shop."

"You are a good man."

"Saber," Illuminado began. "I am *your* man."

"A good man, and a pirate." Saber giggled. "That movie series certainly has influenced my thoughts on the matter."

"Indeed. But I am better looking and stay put longer. There are no beasties after me."

Saber pretended to lift a cup. "I'll drink to that."

"So will I, as soon as our coffees get here. You know, Saber, if you are hungry they can make us lunch. I'm afraid that if we retreat upstairs for paella we will not eat." Illuminado stood as the server brought their French press to the table. "Would you make us some food, my friend?"

"Yes, of course. What would you like?"

Illuminado spoke up. "Olives, cheese, crackers, maybe some of that nice ham. Dried fruit if there's any."

"A charcuterie board, Mr. Constantine? Certainly."

He sat. "Thank you." Then to Saber, "I love my life. I love my staff."

"You don't have charcuterie on the menu board there, *sir.*"

"It's my place. My manager orders the supplies and always gets a few things for me. And my guests."

"Oh, do you bring all your dates here?"

Illuminado laughed. "Oh, please, no. I have brought the custodial staff here and the admins."

"I'm the only date?"

"First and last."

"We barely know each other, but I understand—very deeply—that this might be something big."

Illuminado took her hand across the café table. "I am Spanish on my mother's side. We invented the concept of romantic love. We roved and reeved not simply for conquest, but to express love. Of the sea. Of adventure."

"Not to rain on your parade, but Spanish conquests do not delightful history make."

"Yes, I know. They were arrogant and destructive. But I am not descended from those men. I have the blood of a pirate. For all his faults, and there were many, his descendants have fire in the veins."

"That, sir...I agree with wholeheartedly. We are not that many generations away from our swashbuckling ancestors."

"Which is why we must remain close. We have met under magnificent circumstances, and I believe in love at first sight."

"Pirate to pirate." Saber squeezed his hand.

"Man to woman."

CHAPTER SEVEN

They ate in silence, stealing glances with titillating brushes of fingertips and hands.

"This may be the most interesting date I've ever had," Saber whispered.

"Interesting? Only interesting?"

"All right, how about it is the best date I've had in my adult life. I recall a few childhood escapades of note."

"The first of many."

Saber took his hand. "Why did you get a vasectomy? Were you done having children?"

"I have no children. Nor have I married. When I was a very young man, I enriched a woman. She terminated the pregnancy and I swore I would never allow that to happen again. The doctors have assured me it is fully reversible. Someday, I shall be a father."

"You have got to be the kindest, most thoughtful man ever."

"I am Buddhist. I've been Buddhist since I was twenty. Cause and effect is strict. I make good causes so the effects are positive ones."

"What goes 'round, comes 'round."

Illuminado nodded. "*Sí.*" He paused. "So, we've done all the things today. Should we go to a movie? Bowling? Plunder? Set sail for unchartered waters?"

"Research."

"That is not in the pirate's dating code."

"Did Benito Del Soto ever mix with Anne Bonney? I think they lived a hundred years apart."

"No no no. de Soto began his career in 1828. I believe Anne was dead a hundred years by then."

"Yes. Mid-1700's."

"Well, then Miss MacLean, you and I can be more than passing ships in the night."

"I sometimes have a hard time reconciling things Anne or Calico Jack did with modern sensibilities."

"Benito de Soto most certainly was an unkind man. I will not follow suit. He was not politically motivated. He wanted only riches. And he hurt so many—especially any women he encountered."

"Anne was a clever woman—and a pirate. She fought against imperial rule in the Caribbean."

"Benito raped and pillaged. The myths and legends surrounding him are vast—especially in Gibraltar. But the truth is the truth. He is not so famous in the Caribbean. But in Andalusia, he has quite the reputation. Truthfully, my mother made me swear on the Bible that I would not grow up to be a pirate." He paused, then very thoughtfully, began reciting, "*San Miguel Arcángel, defién-denos en la lucha. Sé nuestro amparo contra la perversidad y acechanzas del demonio. Que Dios manifieste sobre él su poder, es nuestra humilde súplica. Y tú, oh Príncipe de la Milicia Celestial, con el poder que Dios te ha conferido, arroja al infierno a Satanás, y a los demás espíritus malignos que vagan por el mundo para la perdición de las almas. Amén."*

"That's beautiful, but I don't speak Spanish very well."

"Saint Michael the Archangel, defend us in battle. Be our protection against the wickedness and snares of the devil; May God rebuke him, we humbly pray; And do thou, O Prince of the Heavenly Host, by the power of God, thrust into hell Satan and all evil spirits who wander through the world for the ruin of souls. I can say in English, too."

"No wonder you converted to Buddhism."

"*Si.* My altar...it is in my condo. Would you like to see it?" he asked.

Saber nodded. "I guess I was too busy to notice it before." *Too busy!*

"Ah, it is inside the armoire. You may have thought it a television." He stood and held out his arm in escort.

Saber rose and took his arm. She rested her head against his shoulder.

CHAPTER EIGHT

*A*re we going to do it again? I need to brush my teeth. If we continue at this rate I'll be crawling tomorrow.

"Which Buddhism do you practice?"

"Nichiren. The Buddhism of Nichiren Daishonin."

"I know of that. Chanting?"

"*Si.* Often. After we met, I chanted about you, in fact. This magnetic attraction I feel. I would be a fool not to follow the tides of my life." He pulled Saber in for a kiss. "We must explore this relationship thoroughly."

"I'll chant to that," Saber replied.

"You are too perfect, Saber. My last lady friend said she'd pray for me and invited me to her church. And asked me to put GOP flyers in the shop."

"I'm more inclined to Eastern philosophies. And I'm a Democrat."

"I broke it off with her after a short time because we did not see eye-to-eye on anything. She was horrified by my blood ties to a known pirate."

"You are not responsible for the actions of your ancestors. I think we should simply try to live better than they did."

They exited the lift, holding hands. "I built this altar." He motioned to display the armoire.

"I don't recognize the wood."

"It is comprised of strakes from an old sailing vessel. The inlay is Irish bog oak. The handles were hand cast for me in Tangier."

"A dismantled ship repurposed."

"Yes." He opened the armoire doors. "This is my Buddhist scroll." He slid out the top drawer and opened the ends to reveal a breadboard-like shelf upon which was the full accouterment of a Nichiren altar. "We have water, fruit, evergreens, incense, candles, and my prayer book and beads. And my bell...is there..." he nodded to his right.

"And you chant every day. Here."

"I chant everywhere. But this is my primary spot. I pull up a chair and chant as much as I like. Would you like to hear it?"

Saber nodded.

Illuminado retrieved a dining table chair and sat. He ran his bell three times and put his hands together in prayer. "*Nam myoho renge kyo. Nam myoho renge kyo. Nam myoho renge kyo.*" The sound reverberated and filled the room with pure, energetic song.

"I've heard that before—but never so beautifully."

"Thank you."

"Illuminado..."

"Saber?"

"Are we going to be intimate again? Again today? Today as in a few minutes from now?"

"If you wish it, of course. The joys of a new relationship are many. I'm sure there will be a day when wish only to nap."

"Old, in our bed, CPAP and ear plugs if anything like my parents." Saber laughed at her own joke.

"I should be so blessed to wake up to you every morning."

Saber slid her arms around his waist from behind. "You know, Illuminado, we seem to be quite compatible in so many ways, that I feel anxious if I find on some level we do not match."

"I think that is natural, Saber. We must always strive for common ground in our commitment while supporting the growth of the individual."

"Wise, sir."

He turned in her arms and pulled her to him. "I look forward to knowing all about you. To many moonlit nights and birdsong in the early mornings. We shall travel and explore each other and the world."

"You don't have summers off."

"I have plenty of vacation time. Would you like to see Spain? Mallorca? The Canary Islands? Portugal?"

Saber pressed her lips against his and whispered, "Yes."

"We shall go to all these places."

They didn't make love again. The afternoon was spent in lengthy discussions and old-fashioned hand-holding. Saber loved the touch of his hand when he took hers. The energy between them was unmistakable. Undeniable. There were times when she felt like bursting into song. No...bird song. *There are no mortal words to describe what I feel. I...feel good when I'm with him and I'll be damned, I feel better about myself when I'm not. Every irrational fear*

I've ever had is dissipating. He is a balm for heart and soul. He is good medicine.

———

She forced herself to sleep. Her mind was a whir with thoughts of Illuminado, and it took some doing to get her mind still.

It's right. He's right. My great-uncle walked into a millinery shop in France during WWII to buy his mother a pair of gloves. He fell in love, right then, right there, with the woman behind the counter—and she him. She took him home for dinner. He spent the night in their barn. He went to church the next morning with her family. That afternoon, they married. They were together for nearly 60 years. Happily. Very happily. When it's right, it's right. Illuminado Constantine...is right. Uncle Johnny used to say that half the fun of his marriage to Dylette was learning all about her as the days went by. He knew enough after a few hours to know he couldn't live without her. I feel that way.

CHAPTER NINE

Saber drove to work, her belly filled with butterflies. *He is too perfect. I am waiting for the other shoe to drop and the sword to strike. How can this be real? Again, here I am with indecision! Why do I do this to myself? He's so good in bed, and a simple touch of his hand sends me spiraling. Those eyes...his black eyes...pierce me. He can read my soul like a book. I am fucking falling in love. I am in love. Will the students see that we are a thing? Can they smell passion? Middle schoolers are so feral. I wouldn't put it past them to feel the passion in the air between us.*

She shook off her thoughts as she parked. Game face.

She unlocked the staff entrance and walked into the school and directly to her classroom. There, on the counter by her sink, was a single red rose. Nothing else. Just the rose. She reached under the sink for a mason jar and put the perfect bloom into water.

"Good morning, Miss MacLean."

It's him. His aura penetrated her before she even

grasped his words. "Good morning Mr. Constantine. Have a nice weekend?"

He nodded. "Yes. I did, thank you. You?"

She felt her face flush. "Indeed."

"Well," he began, then very quietly said, "I can't hang out here as much as I'd like to. Ring the office if you need me."

I need you! "Yes, thank you." *What can I fucking break or make leak?*

———

I want to kiss her. Now. I want to cup her breasts and feel the curve of her buttocks in those sedate work trousers. She makes me hard with a look. La quiero tan profundamente. Ah, but duty calls. Someday I shall not have to walk away from her. Ella es la única. I've found my match.

District and school policy did not forbid love from taking root—but the principal was against such things having gone through a bitter divorce with a former employee at his school. Though he and Illuminado often shared breaks, there would be no discussing his new love. *Love. Yes. I am falling in love with her. Saber cuts me with a passion as sharp as her name.*

He walked away from her classroom with a smile on his face. *I am normally a happy man. But she...makes me feel so good. Just to look her way. The sight of her.* He shuffled off thoughts of Saber and set his mind on his job. He had daily duties interspersed with minor emergencies, all day —every day. He ducked into one of the custodial closets and sent her a text. "Tonight?"

She responded immediately with a thumbs-up symbol.

He pocketed his phone and went about his day. A day made more glorious by the fact that he would hold the beautiful Saber MacLean later.

CHAPTER TEN

Mr. Brown had a nose for sin. He saw it in telltale signs. Dark circles under the eyes. Clandestine cell usage by staff. Flowers delivered to the school. Giggling hens in the kitchen. Gossipers. Wrapped in utter piousness, he walked with glory and righteousness. After the divorce, Jesus had saved him. Well...not so much Jesus as the preacher. The man of God with whom he now shared faith. Pastor taught the "fine line" principal. Walk the line straight and walk with God. Veer off and fall into sin. It had been quite a life-changing awakening. Men had all the control. Men were the hands of God and women simply needed to cling to them to be filled with the spirit. Taking things back to the good old days...prior to 1960...that's how things had to be to make the USA right again.

So many sins and sinners around him. His office door was closed and locked. He took a nip from the flask in his desk. *They are all going to hell. If only I could save one of them. Even that woman. Put her on the path.* He took another, longer drink, then quickly popped a breath mint.

He had an agenda. Like reciting a Rosary, he ran the list over in his mind.

** Three years of home economics courses for all girls. Cooking, cleaning, sewing. Boys would get one quarter—mostly on how to run a household. Of course, boys would get lessons on gun safety, hunting, wildlands tracking. Important methodologies with which to protect their families before the end times.*

** No more integrated PE. Girls and boys needed to be separated. If I could do that with lunches, I would.*

** Bible study daily for every student. Again, boys and girls separated. Girls needed to hear the Works associated with supporting men, while boys needed to learn how to use God to run the world.*

** Bonuses for every staff member who attended his church.*

** No feminine hygiene products in the restrooms. Menstruating girls would need to report to the school nurse. Keep things tracked. In order. No discussion of birth control. Abstinence and purity would be rewarded.*

Segregation by race would prove more difficult to obtain, but he wanted it. Salivate over it.

By the grace of God, my relations on the board and in the superintendent's office, thy will be done. Soon, laws will be enacted to allow marriage brokers into the schools. The right men will have their choice of girls to wed. Parents will agree to the matches. The revenue to the school system will be tremendous. He paused his lurid thoughts, momentarily, going darker. *I wonder if I can record wedding nights. Perhaps witnesses to the defloration and potential impregnation should be reinstated. Oh, yes. I'd like that. We could pay a bonus to parents who preserve the purity of their daughters. The right men would pay anything just for the opportunity to wed innocence.*

He felt arousal at the thoughts. Because he was a man, and men can stumble, he needed to pray. He caught a glimpse of Saber MacLean walking to class through the two-way window leading to the hall from his office. Strong arousal there. *A comely woman, indeed. Would she submit to me? Or do I need to take what is rightfully mine from her? Women are grateful once they have submitted to a righteous man. There's no reason why I shouldn't have her if I so choose.*

———

The bell sounded at three forty-five and never had Saber been so enthused to finish her day. She glanced at her cell phone, which was safely tucked away during the school day in a locked drawer. Staff and students were forbidden to use them from 8:45-3:45. *His place at 4:30. I can make that.* She had a toothbrush in her purse—and had packed extra clothing in case she stayed the night—in anticipation of the same while fighting back the words and opinions of her mother and grandmother. *Am I going to stay the night? We've done nothing but rut for three days. Should we not ask big questions like what's your credit score? No. We went straight to are you STD-free? He is worth it. I can tell. Is he the one? The one who will hold my cane for me when I bag up green peppers at age eighty? He just might be.*

She loved teaching. But the school, overall, had an aura of depression hovering over it. Like rain clouds that would never dissipate. *Glad to have a job, but glad when I get to leave.* She rang the service bell at the back of the coffee shop. A worker opened the door. She smiled politely and went straight to the elevator. Four-thirty-five. Right on time.

Is he going to be waiting with his dick in his hand? Will desire overtake us before the water for tea has been poured? I hope it's always like this between us. The lift doors whooshed open. Sadly, he was dressed.

"Hello," he said softly. "It's good to see you."

"Hello, Illuminado."

"Would you like a coffee or something stronger?"

Saber chuckled. "I'd like to fuck you." *Sorry, Mom! But this woman isn't going to play hard-to-get or otherwise impede her natural urges. Welcome to the 21st century.*

"Ah, right to it. Perfect!" He slid his arms around her waist, and they kissed deeply. He trailed his kisses down her throat and across her bosom. She wore a light knit hunter green sweater and it fit in all the right places. "I will always want you. I know this."

"Seems odd that the word *always* is springing up in my mind, too."

He slid his right hand up her shirt to cup her breasts, then placed his palm over her heart. "Love at first sight. X marks the heart."

"What's your credit score?"

He choked with laughter. "Really?"

"I was trying to find something...anything...to..." she

paused as he slid a hand between her legs, over her trousers.

"To not love me?" He dropped to his knees before her and unzipped her pants.

"Yes."

"But I am perfect for you, Saber MacLean. Pirate to pirate." He tugged her sedate black slacks down and licked her over her panties.

She couldn't respond. His probing tongue had found its way to her clit and one finger had pressed beyond the silken fabric. He lapped at her and manipulated her lady parts until her panties were soaked. He then pulled them down and buried his face in her labia. He sucked in her clitoris and using two fingers now...he slid them in and out of her wetness until she quaked.

They lay intertwined. Not speaking. Sharing beating hearts. Deep breaths and deeper satisfaction.

"I would like to tell the world of our relationship. How perfect we are for each other."

Saber sighed. "Not at work."

"You are a sub. You will one day leave."

"End of the school year."

"So, we have a few months to remain silent." Illuminado pulled her in tighter. "I have never been a man of patience."

"I'm sure your patience will be rewarded."

"Tell me, my love, how shall we proceed? I am certain that we belong together. And it is not simply because we have great sex and swashbuckler bloodlines. We are immensely compatible."

"I've always been cautious. I have avoided situations such as this."

Illuminado chuckled. "A situation where we are

falling in love and are deeply desirous of making a life together?"

"Yes."

"Saber...don't be afraid. I want to be with you. I'm not saying let's marry next weekend. But we should consider such things. *Si?*" He paused. "You know...we could marry over the weekend."

"Marry?"

"Sir. *Vamos a casarnos.*"

"Are you asking? Officially asking?"

"I'll take you ring shopping if you wish. Do you like such traditions?"

"I do."

Illuminado rolled Saber over and pinned her with kisses. "I am not afraid to love you. My blood boils for you."

Saber gazed into his eyes. "*Sin miedo.*"

"Ah, *en español.* I'm impressed."

She shifted around a bit to have him poised between her legs.

"Would you like me to be further impressed, Saber?" His hardness rested against the apex of her female regions.

She reached her right hand down and guided him into her. "Indeed."

CHAPTER ELEVEN

They made love, ate, and then settled in to watch a movie.

He slipped his arm around her shoulders as the familiar soundtrack to *Pirates of the Caribbean* commenced. "You know, spring break is nigh."

"Nigh? Yes. It is."

"Do you have plans?"

"None, really."

"Do you have a passport?"

Saber nodded.

"Then we shall go to Spain. The Iberian Peninsula. Andalusia. Gibraltar. The city, itself. I have a home there."

"I'm a substitute, Illuminado. I haven't even been paid yet."

"It is no worry. I can afford to take us both and there, we shall find you the perfect ring."

"This isn't moving too fast?" *Uncle Johnny. Think about Uncle Johnny and Dylette. Sixty years together after a thirty-six-hour courtship.*

"I love you, Saber. From the moment our gaze me, I

have loved you. Be mine. Let me be yours. Please, let us wed. My credit score is over eight hundred. Is good, no?"

Wow! "I love you, too. And yes—this is right. I know it's right. I will marry you."

He picked up his phone and opened a travel app. In less than five minutes he had two round-trip tickets to Gibraltar purchased. "All right, we fly out on Saturday morning and return on Friday, so that we have two full days to reacclimate to this time zone."

"I can't believe I'm doing this. Uncle Johnny did it..."

"I do not know Uncle Johnny, but if he loved fast and hard, he and I should be friends. Tell me, Saber MacLean, if you could have a perfect wedding, what would it entail?"

"Casual. Formal clothing is beautiful but not for me. I think I'd rather give the money to charity than spend it all on a wedding and reception."

"Yes. I agree."

"A short ceremony somewhere at sunset followed by dinner and music. Then a smallish reception in a park for family and close friends."

"And someday a family?" he asked softly.

"Yes. Since it appears that fate has drawn us together, would you get a reversal?"

"Of course. And after we have had all the children we wish, I will get snipped again. It is ridiculous to me that women should bear the burden of birth control. I will be your partner in all things."

"And we can't tell a soul."

Illuminado rose and walked around his condo. "No. Not yet."

"I'd like this job to continue. Maybe get a leave replacement contract for next year."

"At my school?"

"Well, yes. But in reality---at any school. Though this district is fast becoming rather religious. I don't want to teach in a parochial school."

"The district does not mind so much when people fall in love, but our principal is very much against it. No fraternization."

Saber pursed her lips. "Then we must be stealthy."

"As pirates."

"Yes."

CHAPTER TWELVE

Illuminado thought he might look the fool pushing around a four-foot dustmop. He couldn't help but smile. He couldn't help but sing softly to himself words of love created by his heart. He deliberately found excuses to travel by room 111 during the day. Saber's pirate-themed room was always awhirl with excited students learning new and wonderful things. *She is an amazing teacher. So animated, vibrant and knowledgeable.*

"Is there a problem with 111, Mr. Constantine?"

The voice grated on him. It was the principal. A broken-hearted man nearing retirement whose family was scattered to the winds and whose wife had run off with another teacher in her school. Resigned their positions and fled to Portugal. His four children were all busy getting their educations or taking care of their own families—in other states. *I don't think he even has a dog.* Illuminado wanted to feel sorry for him. But the man was too bitter. Too damaged. Too inflexible. He found Jesus after his divorce and belonged to a church more restrictive than that southern church that pickets everything they don't agree with.

"Mr. Brown, how are you today?"

"I'm fine. So why do you make hallway sweeps around 111 so many times per day?"

"The drip. I fixed it. I didn't put a work order in for facilities to repair it. I'm just keeping atop my handiwork. Plus this teacher...she uses glitter. I hate glitter."

"Hmmm. I understand about the glitter. But we're supposed to have the plumbers come out for such things."

"Yes. But the district is down to one plumber and is using a contractor as an electrician."

The principal pulled his chin hair. A devilish goatee. "Have you met Miss MacLean?"

"The sub? Yes." *Yes! She is the love of my life!*

"I could swear I saw the two of you walking last weekend?"

"Oh?" Illuminado put his game face on.

"Behind the Beacon. That coffee shop down the street."

"You must be mistaken."

Mr. Brown shrugged. "I hate office romances. The thought of romantic love is a poison of the soul. People should meet someplace like church and have chaperoned dates until marriage. Still, the animal in me sometimes thinks otherwise. I know it's unprofessional of me, but I'd like to buy her a drink. I pray about these feelings. God will strengthen me. If I stumble, I shall be lifted."

Illuminado tightened the grip on his broom handle. "I think thoughts are normal. It is actions that are forbidden."

"Yes." Mr. Brown sighed. "My own rules. For good

reasons. But *mano-y-mano*...I do miss female companion-ship. The Lord has filled my life, though I continue to struggle from time to time. A man needs a wife so that he is not tempted to seek solace elsewhere. Though, men were made to rule and women to submit. I'm sure that, in time, the old ways shall return. After the changes the new president will enforce."

"This is April. The election is in November." Illumi-nado wanted to continue. Try to talk sense into the man. He held his tongue. "I'm sorry for your troubles." *Marital rape? Beatings? Child labor? Oh, Mr. Brown...lo siento mucho.*

"She might be able to alleviate my troubles. Hennessey isn't returning. I could offer her a contract for next year. I wonder how grateful she'd be. She's very smart and attractive in a simple way." He paused. "Oh, I need to submit to the Lord in prayer. I am bearing quite a burden today."

Inappropriate! "I think she has a special someone, sir. I saw him drop her off this morning." *Lies.*

"Ah. Of course. Another promiscuous woman. There are no women left who submit to the Lord in all things. Keep themselves for marriage. Submit to their men. It is so sad. Women can be teachers and nurses—but should cease working once married to care for husband, home, and family." He paused and sighed. "Well, keep it up Illuminado."

"I can do nothing else, sir." *I cannot believe the things that come out of your mouth.*

———

Principal Brown had a mean streak and was at the point in his life where he thought he might need to do something else. Anything else. Work a trawler. Drive a big rig. Education was no longer his bag. Unless things changed drastically and everything became Bible-based, from the curriculum to school uniforms to the roles of women in society—and the age girls were considered women—he was gone. His pastor had a compound of like-minded men and obedient women in Idaho. A refuge for God and country. An army of believers doing the Lord's work.

He found comfort in his Bible and knowledge that he, among all men with whom he was acquainted, was the most righteous. He longed for simpler times. He needed a more traditional life. A wife who dedicated herself to him and the Lord. A home steeped in values he held dear. Like his politics. He loathed living in a blue state.

He didn't generally enjoy time away from work. Breaks were hard. This spring, however, he had a trip planned. Overseas. Something during spring break that might tickle his fancy and give him perspective. He'd met someone on a Christian site...women looking for marriage in a traditional relationship. They were to meet over the break in Europe. She was Ukrainian. Spoke English. Had been raised with the Bible and good, solid traditions. She was twenty and a virgin. He was nearly sixty. It didn't matter. She wanted to get away. Russian soldiers had threatened her.

The bell rang. He knew it was Ms. MacLean's planning period. He strolled into the room as the students filed out.

"Hello, Mr. Brown."

"Hello. Everything going well?"

Saber nodded. "No complaints."

"If you ever need something—you know you can come to me."

"Thank you." Saber shook off a deep uncomfortableness crawling up her arms. "I'm fine. I have everything I need."

"Good. Good. Say...would you like to join me for a cup of coffee sometime? We can talk shop. I think you'll be doing this position for some time. That coffee shop with the lighthouse is nice."

Cringe. "Oh, thank you. But I'm seeing someone. I'm not sure he'd understand if I had coffee with another man. Even my boss."

"Jealous type?"

Hardly. "You don't know the half of it. But he's a good man."

"Well..." the principal paused. "I'll be around." He hoped he was giving her a come-hither look. It had been quite some time since he'd tried to even impress a woman. *I could use an easy woman right now. Maybe that's what I need. Sex. In Biblical times men could take a comely woman to him without all the problems that are associated with it now.*

"Thank you."

Brown walked out as casually as he could. A bit crestfallen but thumbing his phone in his jacket pocket. He had three favorite apps. An adult site that reenacted Biblical relations in detail. Lot's daughters, the angels at Sodom, Song of Solomon. Stoning. Torture. Crucifixion. Much of it came from the Philippines. Fabulous stuff. Then, his dating app and his scriptures. He didn't see a contradiction. He saw only power. And superiority. There were pretty strong policies in place by the district to keep students and staff off such sites, but again...he was the brother of the Sup, cousin to two board members, and had an all-access pass. To everything.

I'll be with my Ukrainian woman soon enough. She has saved herself amidst the hardship of war. She loves Jesus. She wants to make a better life for herself by being a homemaker. Spring break. I meet her during spring break. She's younger... but in her country, older men take younger wives without issue. It will be fine. Everything will be fine. He'd strolled to the office. Always ready to catch the two secretaries sharing photos of grandchildren or pets. That was time wasted which they owed him. He kept track—in his own way. And he would be paid back for those losses... somehow.

He went straight into his office and closed the door. He whipped out his phone and texted Lillya in the app. *I look forward to seeing you and if the Lord is good, we will be together forever as husband and wife.*

She responded quickly. *My ticket has been purchased. Did you get the receipt? I could use some money to make sure my mother is taken care of in my absence.*

Of course. How much?

I think three hundred US dollars would suffice. Things are so expensive here. The war. And other troubles.

I'll send it to you. Thankfully this app provides that service. Be safe.

Lillya sent a smiley face and heart. Principal Brown's heart went pitter-patter. But as that titillation traveled down his body to his groin...he thought of Ms. MacLean.

CHAPTER THIRTEEN

By all the gods, ring! Was it a prayer? Of course, it was a prayer. Friday before spring break...all teachers prayed. The bell dismissal bell rang and the students filed out of the school, a week off and undoubtedly thoughts of non-stop gaming and loafing about on their minds. Schoolwork certainly had not been.

Her bag was packed. It was already in Illuminado's truck. They had a two-hour drive to the airport, then Seattle to Heathrow, Heathrow to Gibraltar. Almost twenty-four hours of travel. First class. A short cab ride to his house. Now looked after by a caretaker—but his. All his.

Ready to jet, her wings were suddenly clipped by Mr. Brown's appearance in her classroom doorway.

"I hope you have a nice break, Saber."

"I will, thank you. I need to catch a flight...if you'll excuse me."

"You're going out of town? Good for you. Though single women shouldn't travel alone these days."

"I won't be alone. Now, I really must..."

"Where are you going?"

"To Europe."

"Oh! So am I! Maybe we can meet up. Will you be near southern Spain?"

"It's a large continent, Mr. Brown. If it's Tuesday it must be Belgum, right? My itinerary is jammed packed."

"Your dance card is full, hmmm? Well, I won't take no for an answer next time. Coffee. All right?"

She nodded and slipped past him. She felt exceedingly uncomfortable as she breezed by and he moved his chest against hers.

She strolled out of the school willing her heart to stillness--and had to pause as she caught sight of him. Dark, swarthy, a sexy five o'clock shadow, clothed in a t-shirt and faded blue jeans. Fucking hot. She smiled and felt herself flush as he returned her smile. *So, this is love. Holy shit. This is love.* "You best get out of this parking lot, sir. I want to kiss you. But the thought of being seen dampers my spirit. Mr. Brown says he's traveling to southern Spain. Can you believe that?"

"Oh, my love...I'm so sorry he wishes to make you into a trad wife. He is a vile man and his beliefs are...detrimental." Illuminado drove his truck out of the parking lot and across the street to a strip mall surrounded by a tall hedge. He put his vehicle into park and pulled Saber into his arms. "Oh, gods. Each time I kiss you it as sweet as the first."

Saber smoothed her hand along his thigh. "Did you forget anything at home? Anything at all?"

He cupped her left breast. "Yes. My orgasm. I left it there."

"We'd better go find it, no?"

"*Si. Quiero en ti.*"

"I don't need to speak Spanish to know what you need. I can see it in your jeans...and feel it inside me already."

"I need to drive, Saber."

She took her hand off his bulge and sat back in her seat. "Do."

He pulled in behind the coffee shop and they made a hasty retreat to his bed.

CHAPTER FOURTEEN

Saber had never flown first class. Illuminado flew nothing but. He was a premier member and the perks...oh...the perks. They breezed through their own private check-in line and were seated on the plane with champagne before she could catch a breath.

"They act like they know you. Personally."

"Welcome to first class. More champagne?" Illuminado laughed. "It is a very long flight and the lights will dim and they'll give us blankets and pillows. I have flown using points alone to New Zealand. I love travel."

"While those in coach flap their wings?"

"Yes. Exactly. That's why the plane is oversold—to make sure there are enough arms to get lift."

Saber rested her head on his shoulder. "I don't feel like I deserve this."

"Oh, my love...you deserve far more."

"I'll pay you back for this."

"I'm sure you could, but please...allow me the courtesy of spoiling you. Men of my country know how to treat women well."

"All right. It is appreciated, Illuminado. I was going to spend spring break petting my cat—who is now being watched by a neighbor."

"I was going to spend spring break at the school, cleaning. My crew is stellar. I left them lists. They'll get it all done. I took vacation time. You are worth every minute. Every expense."

"Have I died and you are an angel?" Her dream of the angel wings swirled in her mind.

"No. I am a man. Your man." He lifted her hand and kissed the underside of her wrist. "Now, rest. I'll wake you when dinner arrives."

Saber snuggled up against him, the armrest up to get closer. A haunting chuckle alarmed her. Reminded her of someone. *There are so many people on this flight...maybe I know someone. Is that Brown? Thank God we are in separate sections of the plane.*

Illuminado reached across and stroked her hair. Comforting her. But he'd heard it, too.

———

Gibraltar was small and crowded. A British colony, everything was in English, followed by Spanish. To catch a cab they had to walk across the tarmac.

"This is really strange. A crosswalk on a runway." Saber very hesitantly made her way to the taxi stand.

"This is Gibraltar. Small, busy. Magical."

"And dangerous. Holy crap, Illuminado. A crosswalk on the runway."

"You will live. I promise. Just wait until we get home."

Illuminado seemed to walk on air with excitement. They took a cab to the house. Built in 1803 it was a snug colonial cottage with a wrap-around veranda, palms, and yucca plants. He had such pride in his voice when speaking of the house. "The outside firepit was built from stones carved from the Rock, itself. The historical society helped the family to carefully remove them from the foundation and preserve them. It is unlawful now to use the limestone."

Saber nodded in agreement. "As it should be."

"The windows are hand-blown glass."

"And your family left?"

"Yes. There's more to the story. Good conversation over a bottle of wine tonight."

"All right."

Entering the house, Saber was instantly struck by the ancient feel of the place. Antiquity. History. The odor of salt spray and leather. No carpet. Cobblestone floors. Wooden plank walls. A pump handle in the kitchen. "This place..."

"It is magnificent, yes. The facilities are updated but have been designed to retain their antiquity."

"This was standing when Benito de Soto lived?"

"Yes. In fact, he lived here for a short time. He was always on the run and never far from the ocean."

"The ocean is so close I can smell it."

"Yes. And the Rock can be seen from the back deck. I was thinking we could go to Morrocco this week, too. It is but a ferry ride away. Less than eight miles."

Saber ran her hands along the rough-hewn stone fireplace mantle. "I love it here."

"Come with me." He took her hand and led her to the back of the house. To the bedroom. The headboard covered one entire wall.

"Holy mother of God."

"Mary will never sleep in this bed—but you…I shall make you call out God's name, over and over. This bedframe…it is so high because warm air rises and though this is a temperate climate, sometimes it can get cold. The fireplace is small."

"Did your parents sleep here?"

He nodded. "Does that bother you? The mattress and bedclothes are new. Even the pillows, too." He stripped off his jeans. "I'm going to shower."

Saber saw the *ensuite* and gasped. "The tile work! Good gods…I've never seen anything like it. Wait…I have. Your condo. It's similar." It reminded her of Roman tile-work unearthed in London. "How old is this tile, Illuminado?"

"The Romans were here in the third century. The tile dates from then. It was uncovered in the backyard when a fence was installed around 1900 and repurposed—and yes, I brought some over for use in my home. I know…it should not have been dismantled, but I cannot fault my ancestors for their vision. There is nothing like Roman glass. Now…take off your clothes. Come into the water with me. Ours was a long flight."

Saber stripped and met him in the ornate tiled shower. They washed…then mashed. They spilled out of the shower and into the bed without drying off. Illuminado buried his face between her legs and lapped from apex to perineum until Saber did, indeed, praise God.

He chuckled as she rode his head until the last vestiges of her orgasm subsided. While she lay wet and panting, he entered her with one thrust. She squirmed under his weight, her vagina sensitive and swollen. It took a minute…but she regained composure and met his body movements.

She didn't think she could come again. Oral sex always gave her the most powerful climaxes and building up to another was rare. Except for today. *He knows me. He's riding high to tease my clit. Oh, gods...yes. I'm going to come again.* She took a deep breath and called her pleasure into the rafters of the 1800's cottage as Illuminado burst inside her. He held the position as he spilled, shuddering.

"With you...each time is better than the last," he whispered. He pulled away, still throbbing. "Look what you do to me."

Saber smirked and reached her right hand between her legs. "You make me wet with need."

"May it always be so."

They drifted off to sleep in each other's arms. "We can nap and adjust to the time difference. Sleep now, my love. Sleep."

CHAPTER FIFTEEN

I n her dreams Saber felt decidedly unsafe. Someone followed her. Coveted her. She pulled her purse closer. As a shadowy figure reached for her, malicious intent wafting out from it like a shield, the wings of an angel enveloped her. Protected her. She bolted upright, holding fast to the images in her dream. "I dreamed of an angel," she relayed.

"Ah, St. Michael visited this place. A great cave is named for him. We can go there. Ancients believed it was the entrance to Hades. Just as the Rock of Gibraltar is one of the Pillars of Hercules. It is walking distance, or we can use the scooter."

"Scooter?"

"Yes. It is in the garage."

"Is it safe?"

"Very."

"St. Michael drove Lucifer from Heaven."

"Yes. That is the legend. The archangel conquered the light bringer. I will never understand this. If you make an offering to the saint in the cave, it is said he will banish a great evil from your life.”

“I’ll keep that in mind.” *I think that’s what I need to do. My dreams—victory over adversity and harm.*

“My love, I’m going to dress and chant and do my evening prayers. Then, we can eat dinner at a stall along the shore and take a nice stroll. Does this work for you?”

Saber nodded. She dressed as Illuminado unpacked his travel Buddhist altar and accoutrement. She walked around the house. The cottage. Two bedrooms. One bath inside and one built off the kitchen. She pumped water into the sink. Out the back door, the Rock loomed. Huge, ancient. Mythic. It appeared as though it was within walking distance. But she knew there would be roads and fences and houses in between her and a momentous climb.

“Well? What do you think of my view?”

“Amazing. You’re finished?”

“I am. Let’s take a walk to the shore. Eat fresh *camarones*. With garlic. And wine. Let’s bring the wine.”

“We can walk with wine?”

Illuminado put on an air of pirate swagger. “Welcome to Gibraltar, love.”

———

“Is that Africa?” Saber turned around to get her bearings. “I can’t believe how clear it is. And only eight miles from here.”

They’d walked along the sandy path for some time. “Ah, you have read about the Strait of Gibraltar.”

Saber nodded and continued. “Let’s see…the Rock is there…which means the other pillar of Hercules is a…”

"Ferry ride away." Illuminado paused. "Just ahead is the best shrimp shack on the straight. Let's take our wine there and have dinner."

Everyone had wine. Everyone. All adults and any children who looked twelve and above...wine. They ordered a basket of steamed shrimp, tails on. It was served with butter and salt. Illuminado poured their wine into plastic cups and dug in. "O *Dios mio*, this is so good."

"*Mi gusta.*"

"Saber, I love it when you speak Spanish. So sexy."

She laughed. "Everyone here speaks English."

"This is true. But we live so close to Spain that we consider ourselves Spaniards."

"You live just as close to Morocco."

"I can walk into Spain. The swim to Morocco is too far. But if you want me to speak French or Arabic, I shall."

"You speak them fluently?"

"I get by. I've been across the straight many times. My mother enjoyed shopping at the souk. She veiled when she went. Just so that the men would not bother her. They pinch and steer foreign women into empty alleys sometimes. I think maybe the country might be more enlightened now, but thirty years ago, not so much. She was fluent in both Arabic and French."

"Your poor mother."

"Remember...my mother had the blood of a pirate and she could defend herself. Truthfully, she and my father shared a lineage—and were distant cousins. They didn't like it when I called the family *Benito Spawn*."

"A pirate bookkeeper. Well...a custodial pirate, so why not?"

Saber tried not to make little happy noises while eating the shrimp. "This is so good."

"Fresh. Everything here is fresh. It's a world apart. Though we are a part of Europe, we are unique. Gibraltar is magical."

"I'm beginning to feel that."

"So...Morocco. Portugal. Spain. After we see the sites here...where shall we go?"

"We have six days. Everywhere?"

"As you wish, my love. What about the top of the rock, with a priest?"

"Get married? Don't we need a license or something?"

"Maybe. But we can do formalities back home. Let's get the padre from St. Michael's cave, take the tram up to the top of the rock, and say our vows. Well...we cannot get to the true highest peak any longer. But there is a skywalk that overlooks the straight. That will do. Saber... will you marry me?"

She smiled. "Yes. I will."

"Do not think this is too quickly to happen or that it might be a mistake. We belong together."

"Will we have to keep this secret?"

"From Brown? Maybe. A married couple might be less of a threat to him than unmarried lovers. Although I think he wants you."

"I've felt that. He is creepy. He looks at me like I'm an ice cream melting in the sun and he needs to lap me up as quickly as possible."

"I think the staff complained about him to their union rep. He may be moved. But with his connections, his abuses and odd insistences may continue."

"I need my job."

"Yes. And a continuing contract next year."

Saber nodded.

Illuminado picked up his cell phone and quickly sent a text. "I will check with the padre now."

"He's in your phone?"

"He's my cousin."

"Of course, he is."

"I will add you to my insurance once we have signed the license. We can wed tonight and pick up the papers tomorrow. It is a simple process here."

"Sounds lovely."

His phone chirped. "Ah, we can we tonight after the last tram. Around 9:30 or 10:00."

Saber laughed. "So fast. We are moving so fast. But I say yes. Let's."

"There are shops nearby. Let us find rings."

———

"Is this ruby?" Saber marveled at the flash and glow of the ring presented to her.

"No. It is red beryl. Very rare. The smaller stones are andalusite."

"Is this the ring you shall wear to represent our love, Saber?"

"It is."

The jeweler spoke English, but Illuminado completed the transaction in Spanish. "*Le queda muy bien. Lo tomaré. ¿Puedes cargar a mi patrimonio?*"

"Yes, Mr. Constantine. Certainly. It is lovely on your hand. And if I may be the first to call you thusly: Mrs. Constantine."

Saber blushed. "Thank you."

"I will take a plain braided silver ring. Preferably

made in the north of Spain." Illuminado scanned the display cases. "This one will do."

"Yes, sir. Shall I also bill this to the estate?"

Illuminado nodded.

"Saber...we have the rings. I tell you...it will be windy atop the Rock. Do you wish a dress, or perhaps a parka?"

"Is it that cold?"

"Windy. Very windy."

"I'll be fine."

"Had we planned a bit more ahead of time we could have reserved the chapel. Mons Calpe Suite. It is a beautiful venue at the top of the tram. We can have dinner there this week sometimes."

"It's very exciting. We can make offerings at St. Michael's cave beforehand."

"After, I think. We should leave a nice bottle of cognac and flowers."

"He is a priest who appreciates a good bottle of cognac?"

"Yes. Well...those who glean the offerings do."

Saber slipped her arm inside Illuminado's and followed him from the shop, admiring the flash of her ring. "All right, lover, lead away."

The evening crowd was nearly elbow-to-elbow in certain areas, but Illuminado guided them safely to a liquor store. "For St. Michael," he said to the shopkeep.

"Ah, no shortage of fortified wine for the archangel. Take your pick, my friend. Or have your lovely lady friend choose."

"Oh, well...I'd go with the one with the dragon on the label. Definitely."

The clerk bagged the bottle and took Illuminado's card. "Be quick now. The last cable car is at 9:00 p.m."

"We can take a taxi." He took Saber's hand and led her into the throng of people milling about the warm evening air. He hailed a cab and they climbed in. "The Reserve entrance, please."

It wasn't far. The foot traffic was a bit hectic, but the driver apparently knew how to avoid humans and the famous Barbary monkeys seeking handouts.

"Are they mean? Those monkeys?"

The cabbie pulled up at the entrance to the nature reserve. A half-dozen Barbary macaques jumped around.

"Do not feed or touch the monkeys, Saber. It is almost $5,000.00 U.S. in fines."

"Are you fucking kidding me?"

The cab driver laughed. "I would not test the rule, madam. Your gentleman friend speaks the truth."

Illuminado handed the man a fist full of cash and they exited. It was late.

They dashed to the tram and Illuminado flashed a card at the operator. "I ride for free," he whispered.

"Because your father ran the thing?"

"Yes."

But a few minutes later they reached the cable car top station and holding hands, trekked the short distance to the skywalk bridge.

"Padre!" Illuminado called as his cousin rushed to meet them.

"Illuminado. And this is your betrothed, Saber?"

"Yes, Father. I'm the one crazy enough to marry him."

"It is late, so we must make haste. I will officiate in the center of the bridge overlooking Spain, Gibraltar, and Morocco. Nado, I know you are no longer Catholic. Should I amend the ceremony?"

"No, do what you do. We just wish to wed atop the Rock."

"Alas, we cannot climb to the top like when we were children with a bottle of stolen port and toast Hercules."

Saber pulled Illuminado's arm. "You did what?"

"Later. Later, my love. Rico and I were reckless youths. Full of mischief."

Father Rico laughed. "Do not worry over the errors of our youth. Illuminado is a good man. Why, he is a major benefactor to several charitable causes here. But someday ask him about our time spent at his mother's home in La Linea."

Illuminado leaned in and whispered to Saber as they walked, "Coffee house money. I make donations. And we were never arrested."

"And from your wayward youth, you became a priest?"

"I always knew I was to serve the church. But yes, I certainly ran amuck a bit. Shall we begin?"

Illuminado took Saber's hand in his. "My love."

She smiled. *How can I not smile at this man?* "My love." The skywalk was glass. Thick glass. Transparent and frightening. "There are monkeys on the bridge."

"Usually, yes. Let's make our way to the center and then please, join hands."

Illuminado and Saber bypassed the macaques without incident and walked with Father Rico to the middle of the bridge.

Rico began. "Let's make short work of this so that you can go to the cave before it closes. I will meet you at the registrar's office tomorrow and sign the forms." He paused. "Before God and witnessed by the majesty of

Gibraltar, Spain, and Morocco, do you, Illuminado Constantine, take this woman as wife?"

"I do."

"Madam, before God and witnessed by the majesty of Gibraltar, Spain, and Morocco, do you, Saber MacLean, take this man as husband?"

"I do."

"Please, Nado, place the ring on Saber's ringer and say *with this ring I thee wed.*"

Illuminado laughed. "She is already wearing my ring. But yes. With this ring, I thee wed, my beautiful Saber."

Rico chuckled. "He is already wearing his ring, yes?"

Saber nodded. "With this ring, I thee wed."

"May your marriage be blessed by Our Lord and watched over by St. Michael who watches over Gibraltar and those who visit the grotto. I pronounce you husband and wife. You may kiss."

And they did. Deep, long...the most heartfelt kiss either had ever shared with another. Sparks flew. In the Strait, barges paused. Ship bells rang. Macaques danced with the stars appearing above them.

"Congratulations, cousins. There's just enough time for you to visit St. Michael's Cave. You can thank him for bringing you together. He is always triumphant."

Saber held Illuminado tightly. "Let's."

"Yes, Rico. We shall go now. We have cognac and flowers to leave at the altar. It should be good now since it is so late and I see few tourists. Thank you, cousin. You look good in your vestments. I will always remember you a mostly naked boy stealing sweets, however."

"It was hot. I was hungry. Now go, you two. May God bless you."

"Thank you, Father." Saber took a deep breath and walked along the glass sky bridge, holding fast to the railing. Beneath her feet were only rocks and sea. She did not look up but kept her vision focused on the slabs of glass. *Don't crack. Don't crack.*

St. Michael's Cave was close. The usual throng of tourists had dissipated as night fell.

Illuminado led her. "We can return and walk the Mediterranean Steps if you wish. It is quite the hike, but worth it for the view. When I was a child we could climb the fence and hike to the top of the north peak. No longer. Now it is forbidden. But I will say that marrying you on the skywalk was amazing. We stood under the heavens with three countries before us."

"I will treasure the memory. Right now, I'd like to get home after the cave. It's our wedding night."

Illuminado patted her rear end. "I will make love to my wife tonight."

They purchased tickets and entered St. Michael's Cave through a well-marked entrance. The last tour group was exiting and the vestibule was nearly empty.

"There are no words," Saber marveled. The entrance was hand-hewn and teemed with the essence of thousands of pilgrims and tourists. Reflecting lights and music filled the vault. Cascading rivulets of light resembling a waterfall and butterflies graced the stone walls. A natural rock formation resembling the wings of an angel was highlighted in brilliant pastel tones. "St. Michael?"

"Yes."

"This place is beautiful."

"And huge. The tunnels carved in WWII riddle this place like Swiss cheese. Much of it is off-limits to tourists. Only locals know of the offering table. Let us go there now. I promise we can return to the cave for the tourist show."

He led her through and around the myriad of steps and lights until they dipped through a low arch and into an area untouched by the high-tech glamor of the attraction. "My love, I must use the facilities. Please… there is nothing to leaving the offerings and saying a prayer, no?"

"I got this…Nado. See you in a little bit."

Illuminado wandered away as Saber looked at the stone slab used for offerings to St. Michael. There were a few half-dried bouquets and two bottles of wine. Sadly, a pair of baby shoes. And a cat collar.

She set her bottle on the table and knelt on the riser. She folded her hands in prayer. And suddenly felt crowded. Uncomfortable.

"Oh, I'm sorry, miss. But you…" a soft male voice whispered. "You are Saber MacLean. Yes. It is you."

She turned her head slightly. And held her breath. "Principal Brown."

"Well, fancy this."

"Yes."

"Are you alone, Miss Evangelista?"

She shook her head.

"I came here to pray. Will you pray with me?" Brown asked. "My pastor told me of this shrine to St. Michael and told me how to find this altar in the midst of all this commercialism."

"I just came to leave traditional gifts. The cabbie told me about it."

He reached out and touched her arm. "You know, in a few days, I will be married. I'm meeting my betrothed tomorrow in La Linea. She flew in from the Ukraine."

"You're getting married?" Saber rolled her shoulder away from his touch.

"A man needs a good woman."

Saber didn't reply. *Where the hell is Illuminado?*

Brown continued. His breath stank like whiskey. "But a man also needs release. And it is not forbidden for me to hold another woman before I wed." He leaned in to kiss Saber.

"No, please don't." She stood.

"We are here now—is this not divine intervention? I must admit I have wanted you since you were hired. I find you most attractive. I know you are not pure. Illuminado said you had a boyfriend. I don't care. Let me have you, Saber. Let me fuck you." He emphasized the word *fuck* as if it were a privilege.

"No."

He didn't accept her answer and slammed her against the altar table, ripping open her shirt. "I must have you. I am dominant and you must submit to me. It is God's way."

"No!" Saber brought up a knee and slammed him in the groin. "It may be God's way, but it is most certainly not my way, nor is this even legal. What the hell is wrong with you?"

"I like it rough. My wife knows and she wants to be dominated."

He turned her, bent her over the table, and lifted her skirt.

Saber screamed. "I'm married. Stop!"

His hand smashed against her mouth and nose. In the short breaths she could obtain, she smelled tobacco and booze. And sweat. She fought against him as he fumbled to unzip his pants with his left hand. She felt his bitter hardness against her. He pinched her nose and pressed harder against her face. She saw stars as oxygen fled. She hit him. She struggled desperately to free herself as unconsciousness enveloped her.

And then he was gone. Pulled from her. Lifted off her. She gasped and filled her lungs with air. Saber defiantly punched at the air, until she saw Illuminado holding Brown by his shirt collar. His muscled arms and strong stance were firm. Resolute. "Leave her alone. How dare you assault my wife!"

Saber pulled herself together and approached Brown. "That's right, you son of a bitch. We're married." She let fly her right fist and hit her principal squarely in the jaw.

Illuminado held his closed fist aloft and it quivered as he used all his strength not to bring it down against Brown. "You know there are cameras everywhere in this place. Not only have you been witnessed by them, but St. Michael. And he is known to defeat evil. And Mr. Brown, you are evil."

"Illuminado...please unhand me. We can forget this. I don't know what came over me."

"Saber, call 999 and ask the police to respond. We take attempted rape and physical battery very seriously in Gibraltar."

"I cannot be arrested. I'll lose my job. I'll lose Lillya."

Illuminado released Brown and spat. "You are lower than the dust. You are evil and corrupt. Retire. Move away."

"Yes."

Saber continued. "St. Michael is said to have cast out the devil. Well, here we are, casting you out, too. Leave. Stay here with your mail-order bride."

"I will. Please, I will leave."

"Do you not wish to apologize for your behavior toward my wife?"

"I don't know what came over me."

Saber poked his shoulder. "You said that, asshole."

"I'm sorry, Miss MacLean. So sorry."

Saber felt her hand curl into a fist again and let it fly. She struck Brown so hard that he fell over. "Mrs. Constantine. I'm so sorry, Mrs. Constantine."

Brown burst out crying. "Mrs. Constantine."

"Get the fuck out of here," Illuminado commanded.

Brown picked himself up and scurried away into the light show of the sacred area.

"Are you all right? Do we need a doctor?" Illuminado asked, cradling Saber in his arms. "You have quite the right fist."

"Brothers. Twin brothers, two years younger. Lots of practice. And I'm fine. Oddly, or not so oddly, it's not the first time I've fought off an attacker. Some men think they have a right to a woman's body."

"They should be hanged."

"Or re-educated."

"Let me help you straighten your clothing and let's go home."

Supporting her, though he knew his assistance was probably not needed, Illuminado led Saber into the main chamber. As they descended a staircase, the stalactites said to be the wings of an angel high above them, lit up. Rich blue turned to green then yellow followed by a brilliant white.

"My dream."

"What my love?"

"I dreamed of an angel's wings in a time of adversity."

"Although I am no longer Catholic, I believe in the

power of angels. Protective functions of the universe. St. Michael has protected you from evil. It is his job."

"Thank you, St. Michael!"

They walked carefully out of the cave and to the entrance to the preserve. Illuminado had an Uber meet them.

CHAPTER SIXTEEN

Brown fled St. Michael's Cave, humiliated, ego-bruised and bashed. He took a cab to La Linea where he hoped Lillya would await him.

I can never return to work. Is this my sign to retire? Resign?

He needed to make an immediate decision. Now. Yes.

I have to make amends.

He hopped out of the cab at the appointed place and quickly texted his brother, the superintendent.

Dear God, why did you allow me to go so far astray?

"I am resigning effective immediately. I will process my retirement upon my return from Europe. Please appoint the assistant principal as interim and in Hennessey's absence, give Miss MacLean a continuing contract. Thank you."

He knows I was considering this. It should not come as a surprise. May the Lord forgive me for my arrogance.

Brown then texted his pastor. "

I will be leaving your church effective immediately. I love Jesus, but not the values you espouse. Do not contact me further."

He spotted Lillya. She ran to him. "Phillip!"

Former principal Brown wasn't sure how to tell his intended that he no longer had the lucrative administrative position and that he had resigned from it because he tried to rape one of his teachers in a fit of male misogyny brought on by the teachings of his pastor and extremely right-wing church. *I won't mention that right now. She is lovely, but she's definitely older and she doesn't have the continence of a virgin. I think I really don't care at this point.*

Crestfallen, he put on a happy face.

Lillya needed this man. He was her ticket out of a warzone. A ticket for her and her family. Even though he looked like he had just been through a battlefield. *Does he realize how disheveled he looks? Still, he was handsome for an older man. His shoulders are hunched over as if he is troubled. I can fix this.* All I have to do is get to America with him, seal the deal, have his baby, and bring my family over. It is nice to finally meet you face-to-face Phillip You as well, Leah.

"Lillya, it's so nice to meet you. Have you checked into our hotel? I did get separate rooms. For now."

"Yes, thank you. Philip, were you mugged? Is that the correct word?"

"No. But we need to talk. The last few hours have been trying. Revealing. Cathartic. I've made some mistakes. I am remedying them. Prayer would be helpful. Will you pray with me?"

She looped her arm in his and they departed for their

hotel. "Yes. We shall pray. There is nothing too large for God."

"I left my church, Lillya. The pastor's teachings are deceptive and I was led to believe things that are simply incorrect. I'm going to retire, too."

"Will you have money to support us? My family?"

Brown sensed the concern in her voice. "Yes. My retirement is substantial. We'll be fine."

"Philip, we shall never again speak of the things bothering you today. Humble yourself before the Lord and I will help you make amends and do your penance."

"Lillya, will you marry me?" he asked.

She nodded. "Yes."

CHAPTER SEVENTEEN

Saber checked a text message ping. "Holy shit."

"What?"

"It is from Brown. He has resigned. He has instructed the assistant principal to hire me for the next school year because Hennessey is not returning. He resigned his contract, too."

"Wow."

"He's leaving and I'm staying."

Saber read aloud. "I will instruct the admin assistant to label your mailbox S. Constantine. Please forgive me my transgressions against you." She laughed. "Try attempted rape, asshole. This is a huge win, Illuminado. And although I just fought off an attacker from sexually assaulting me seemingly because he believes it was his Biblical right...this is our wedding night. I refuse to let him ruin it. Let's go home."

"I love you, Saber. I will love you forever."

"And I you."

EPILOGUE

She pushed her walker ahead of her, catching her reflection in the shiny mirrors of the produce backsplash. A fine mist wafted out from the vegetables. She chose a brilliant verdant green pepper. Before she could reach above her head for a bag, one appeared before her.

"Thank you, darling."

"Of course, *mi amor*. It will be a lovely 40th anniversary dinner. Married all these years and I love you more now than I did when first I saw you in the staff room."

"Retiring early and moving to Gibraltar was a brilliant move. These years have been so enjoyable with our children growing up in the shadow of the Rock. Our travels... oh, Illuminado...the places we've seen."

"Yes. And places we've made love."

"That never grows old." Saber leaned in, over her walker, to kiss her husband.

"And now that your hip is new, we shall have more adventures. We are only in our 80's after all. So much life yet to live."

"I look forward to the rest of my time with you here, and can't wait for our next lifetime together, Mr. Constantine."

"Pirate to pirate," he replied. "Pirate to pirate."

98

ABOUT THE AUTHOR

Join Darragha's mailing list:

Darragha Foster is an award-winning and best-selling author of paranormal romances who finds inspiration all around her. Including the cold case at the grocer's, where she is no longer welcome.

Spice and Sass.

She also writes under JJ Andrews.

www.authorjjandrews.com